For Caleb, Aidan, Kellan, Ethan,
and Quinn—all cool guys!
—T.A.

ISBN 978-1-338-87567-6

10 9 8 7 6 5 4 3 2 1   22 23 24 25 26

Printed in the U.S.A.   40

This edition first printing, 2022

A boy had a pet fly.
He named him Fly Guy.
Fly Guy could say
the boy's name—

BUZZ!

FLY GUY

<u>Chapter 1</u>

One day, Buzz and
Fly Guy went outside.

"Let's play hide-and-seek,"
said Buzz.

Fly Guy hid
in the garbage can.
He always hid
in the garbage can.

He liked to eat while
Buzz looked for him.

"I spy Fly Guy!" said Buzz.
"It's my turn to hide."

Buzz hid in the garden shed and shut the door.

Fly Guy found a way in.

"You are GOOD!" said Buzz.
"It's your turn to hide again."

Fly Guy hid in
the garbage can again.

Just then, the
garbageman came.

He dumped the garbage
into the truck and drove away.

Chapter 2

Buzz's dad was going
to work.

"Follow that truck!"
cried Buzz.

The truck drove and drove
and drove, all the way
to the town dump.

Buzz ran into the dump.
"Fly Guy, where are you?"

"Fly Guy," he cried.
"Answer me!"

A zillion flies all answered,

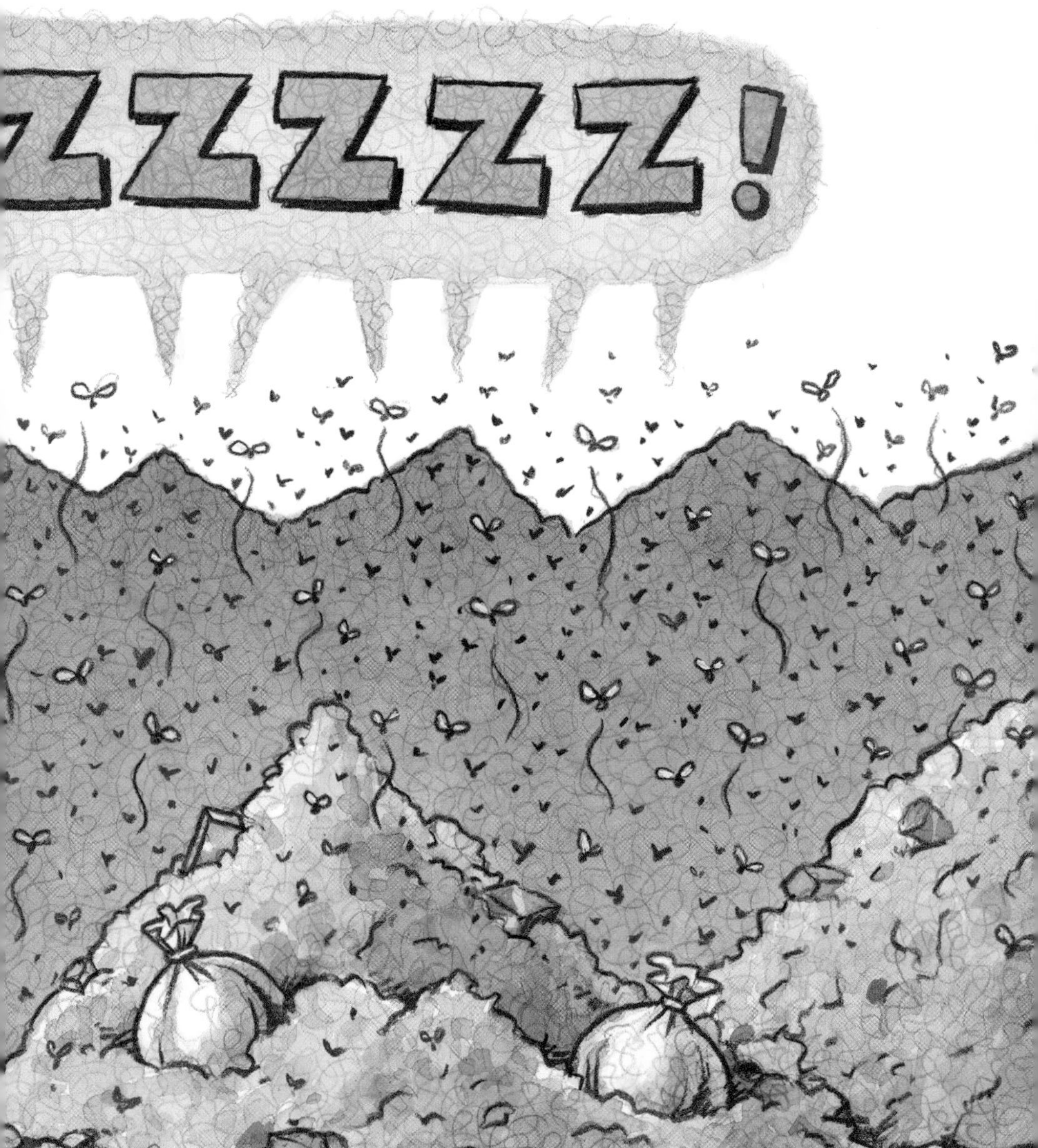
ZZZZZZ!

"Oh, no!" cried Buzz.
"They all can say my name!
How will I find Fly Guy?"

Buzz spied a fly hiding.
"Do I spy Fly Guy?"
The fly flew away.

Buzz spied a fly eating.
"Do I spy Fly Guy?"
The fly boinked him
on the nose and flew away.

Buzz spied a fly landing
on his hand.
"Do I spy Fly Guy?"
The fly bit him and flew away.

Chapter 3

Buzz was sad.

Was Fly Guy gone forever?

He kicked a can.
He kicked a jar.

Then Buzz remembered.
They were still playing a game.

"Okay, Fly Guy," yelled Buzz,
"I give up. You win."

He heard a voice from above.

"I SPY FLY GUY!"
cried Buzz.

And Fly Guy said,